Sally Noll

LUCKY
MORNING

Greenwillow Books, New York

*Library of Congress Cataloging-in-Publication Data
Noll, Sally.
Lucky morning / by Sally Noll.
Summary: While on vacation in the mountains of Montana,
a young girl and her grandfather share a special morning.
ISBN 0-688-12474-7 (trade).   ISBN 0-688-12475-5 (lib. bdg.)
[1. Grandfathers—Fiction.   2. Vacations—Fiction.]   I. Title.
PZ7.N725Lu   1994   [E]—dc20   93-18188   CIP   AC*

For my father, with absolute love

Every summer in June Nora's grandma and granddaddy went to Montana for one week.

This summer Nora went along, too.

Granddaddy loved fishing, and on his first morning there he went to the river. Nora went with him. She wore boots and carried his basket.

"Good luck," called Grandma from the porch. "Be back for lunch."

And off they went down the road.

"It looks as if someone wants to say hello to us,"
said Granddaddy as they passed the Taylor Ranch.

"She's beautiful," said Nora.
"And so is her colt!" said Grandaddy.

"Do you think we will see any *wild* animals?" asked Nora as they walked past the buttercup meadow.
"There's a chance," said Granddaddy.

"Why, just look up there," said Granddaddy as they went by Bear Mountain. "Can you see what I see?"

"Do you think we will see a *real* bear?" asked Nora.
"There's a chance," said Granddaddy.

"Look at those clouds,"
said Granddaddy
as they turned off
toward the river.
"Can you see
what I see?"

"Do you think we will see a *real* moose?" asked Nora.
"There's a chance," said Granddaddy.

At the river Granddaddy settled into
a morning of fishing.

Nora settled into a patch of clover.

As time passed, she decided to try
and find one with four leaves.

I wonder if I can, she thought to herself.

"Look what I found!" cried Nora.

"Eureka!" shouted Granddaddy at the same time.
"There's a tug on my line!"

"This was a lucky morning, wasn't it, Granddaddy?" said Nora. "My clover brought you a fish."

"The day is still young, my angel," said Granddaddy. "Your clover may have more luck to bring us, but right now let's head back for lunch. I'm as hungry as a moose."

And off they went down the road.

"Hush," whispered Granddaddy as they headed away from the river. "Can you see what I see?"

They stared and waited. Then they walked on quietly.

"Hush," whispered Grandaddy as they passed by Bear Mountain. "Can you see what I see?" They watched in silence. Then they walked on quietly.

"Hush," whispered Granddaddy as they passed the buttercup meadow. "Can you see what I see?"
They looked, then walked on quietly.

When they came to the Taylor Ranch, Granddaddy said, "This was a lucky morning."

"A very lucky morning," said Nora. "I can't wait to tell Grandma about everything."

"Do you think we have seen all the wild animals
that good luck will bring?" asked Nora.
"Not a chance," said Granddaddy.